LONELY LAMB

Other Books in the
ANIMAL EMERGENCY *Series by*
Emily Costello

LONELY LAMB

EMILY COSTELLO

ILLUSTRATED BY LARRY DAY

AVON BOOKS
An Imprint of HarperCollinsPublishers

To Marian Eide and Sadie

ACKNOWLEDGMENTS

The author wishes to thank Rex and Susan Mongold of Tongue River Farm in Montana and Grace Gerber of Larkspur Funny Farm in Colorado for sharing their knowledge of how sheep survive when winter winds blow. Thanks also to Lex and Marty Becker, who told me the amazing story of their three-legged dog "Lllucky Boo."

LONELY
LAMB

• 1 •

"Come on, Chewy!" Stella Sullivan clapped her hand against her thigh. She ran sideways across the frozen ground toward the back door of the animal clinic. In the cold air, her breath came out in white billows.

Chewy, a big sheepdog, nipped at her heels in excitement. He ran as fast as Stella did, which made her smile broaden.

Anya did a good job on Chewy, Stella thought. *No matter what his owner thinks.*

A few weeks earlier, Chewy had been hit by a car. His right rear leg had been crushed. Stella's Aunt Anya, the town veterinarian, had to amputate—to cut off—the leg. Chewy's owner didn't want a three-legged dog, so the dog had been living at the animal clinic.

Stella led Chewy up the back steps and into the clinic's boarder room. His pink tongue was hanging way out of one side of his mouth.

"Want some water?" Stella asked the dog. She went to the sink and filled a green plastic dog dish.

Stella put the bowl on the concrete floor and Chewy began to lap it up. "This is your last night here," Stella told the dog. "Tomorrow you start your new life."

Chewy was going to live on a sheep farm. The farm belonged to a friend of Stella's grandfather. Papa Pete and Stella were going to drop the dog off the next day. Stella was not looking forward to spending the morning with her grandfather. He made her grumpy and she made him even grumpier.

Chewy paid no attention to Stella. He lapped at the water, flinging half of it onto the floor.

As Stella reached for a paper towel, she heard someone come into the room. She turned and saw Marisa Capra standing at the door.

Marisa was a friend from school. She was a pretty girl with thick brown hair and hazel eyes framed by long dark lashes. Right now, her face was shiny with tears.

"What's wrong?" Stella asked.

"It's Merlin," Marisa said in a shaky voice.

"Your new cat?" Stella asked.

Marisa sniffled and nodded. Stella knew Marisa had gotten the cat for Christmas. Marisa's parents had rescued the kitty from the pound in Billings.

"I never had a cat before," Marisa said sadly. "I didn't know . . ."

"What happened?" Stella asked.

"He ate tinsel off the Christmas tree." Marisa's mouth turned down, her eyes squeezed shut, and her shoulders started to shake. "I should have watched him better," she choked out.

"Don't cry," Stella said as she put an arm around her friend's shoulders. "Rufus is always trying to eat weird stuff like socks and garbage. So far it hasn't hurt him." Rufus was Stella's little dog. He was good at getting into trouble.

"Could you find out what's going on?" Marisa asked.

"Sure," Stella said. She put Chewy in his cage. She and Marisa went down the hall. When they got to the door of Exam One, Marisa kept going toward the waiting room. Stella pushed the exam room door open and walked quietly inside. She knew Anya wouldn't mind.

Anya was standing at the stainless steel table,

holding a big gray cat with one hand. She used her other hand to massage his belly.

Merlin was fluffy and fat. He looked at Stella with sad yellow eyes. He wasn't enjoying his exam, but he made no attempt to escape.

Anya gave Stella a brief smile, but her eyes lost their focus as she concentrated on the exam.

"Marisa told me," Stella said as she came up beside the table and stroked Merlin between the ears. "Is he going to be okay?"

Anya shrugged. "Tinsel can cause all sorts of problems. If one end passes into Merlin's intestine while the other end is stuck in his stomach, the tinsel could slice through his bowels like a knife and release poisonous digestive juices."

Stella bit her bottom lip. She'd assumed Marisa was overreacting. Marisa's mom, Mrs. Capra, was always dragging Anya out to their place for the silliest reasons—like the time she thought her seven-hundred-pound sow had a sunburn. But it sounded as if Merlin was really sick.

"We could wait and see if Merlin poops out the tinsel," Anya said thoughtfully. "Or I could operate now."

Stella could hear the hesitation in Anya's voice. "Normally I like to give cats a chance to pass foreign objects," Anya continued. As she talked, she took hold of Merlin's head and pushed up his lip so she could see his teeth.

Merlin reacted with a lazy blink.

"I could wait a few days and do the operation if I see signs of distress," Anya added.

Stella nodded. She knew Anya always avoided operating if she could. "That way you don't have to risk putting him under, right?" she asked.

"Yeah," Anya said. "Operations can be hard on kitties. And Mrs. Capra doesn't know how old Merlin is. Judging from the wear and tear on his teeth, I'd say he's at least eight. Maybe older."

"So we should wait," Stella said.

"Yes, except . . ." Anya still hesitated. "In this case, I think I may operate right away."

"Why?" Stella asked.

"The Capras," Anya said with a sigh. "I'm not sure they can handle several days of wait-and-see."

Stella stepped back in surprise. "You mean you'd operate just to keep Marisa and Mrs. Capra from worrying?"

"Those two are so emotional about their animals," Anya said with a weary shake of her head. "Remember when one of their goats scratched her eye?"

Stella nodded briskly. "Sally."

"Sally—right," Anya said. "Mrs. Capra slept in the barn until her eye healed."

"So?" Stella said.

"So I'd like to spare Mrs. Capra several days of worrying," Anya said.

Stella stared at Anya, shocked by what her aunt was suggesting. "You can't operate just because Mrs. Capra is a crybaby," Stella said. "You have to do what's right for Merlin!"

"Most of my job is doing what's best for the animals," Anya disagreed gently. "But I also have to consider the owners. People matter, too."

Stella looked at Merlin, sitting patiently on the exam table. He was licking one paw and using it to smooth down the fur on his face. Stella scratched behind his ear and he began a low rumbling purr.

Merlin was old. An ordinary gray cat. Only someone who loved animals as much as Mrs. Capra would have adopted him. Mrs. Capra probably chose him precisely because he *was* so ordinary. She'd probably worried that nobody else would want him. Mrs. Capra had given Merlin a home. But, still, it didn't seem right to operate on him just to save Marisa and her mom some anxiety.

Stella put one hand on her chest. "Trust me," she pleaded. "I can handle Marisa and her mom. When they call a hundred times to check up on

Merlin, I'll answer the phone. Winter vacation doesn't end until next week. He's such a sweet kitty. Don't operate on him if you don't have to."

Anya stared at Stella for a long moment.

Stella sensed that her aunt was weakening. "Please?" she said.

"All right," Anya said, suddenly making up her mind. "Come on. You can help me talk to them."

Anya put Merlin back into his carrier. She put a hand on Stella's shoulder and led her toward the door.

Mrs. Capra and Marisa were sitting next to each other in the waiting room. Their shoulders were touching and they were poised on the very edge of their seats.

"Is he okay?" Marisa asked.

Anya grabbed a chair, pulled it closer to the Capras, and sat down. Stella leaned against the side of her aunt's chair and gave Marisa an encouraging smile.

"Ingesting tinsel is potentially quite serious," Anya began. "The tinsel could injure Merlin's bowel. That could be a life-threatening condition."

Mrs. Capra drew her breath in sharply. "Life-threatening?" she repeated, grabbing her chest.

"Potentially," Anya emphasized.

Marisa's eyes flooded with tears.

"I want that tinsel out of my baby cat," Mrs. Capra said. "Do whatever you have to do. Just make him better."

Anya shot Stella a look and then took a deep breath. "We may need to operate to remove the tinsel. But I'd like to give Merlin a chance to pass it first."

"Isn't waiting risky?" Mrs. Capra asked.

"There is some danger," Anya admitted. "But operations are tough on older cats. I think it would be best to wait and keep our fingers crossed."

"I won't sleep a wink until Merlin is better," Mrs. Capra announced.

Anya nodded slowly and smiled. "I considered that."

"Well, I'm sure you know best . . ." Mrs. Capra said uncertainly.

"Do we have to leave Merlin here?" Marisa asked.

"Definitely," Anya said.

"I'll keep an eye on him," Stella put in. "And I'll call you if anything changes."

The Capras got up, pained and uncertain, and headed for the door. Marisa looked back. She held up her hand to show Stella that her fingers were crossed.

"Try not to worry," Stella said. "I'll call you and let you know if anything happens."

Anya sighed as the door closed behind the Capras. "Go upstairs and get some soft bread," she told Stella. "Soak a slice in milk and feed that to Merlin. The bread may coat the tinsel and help it pass through his bowel without doing any harm."

"Okay!" Stella agreed. She ran up the steps to the second floor, and raced into Anya's apartment. She took a bowl out of the cabinet, and added bread and milk.

She smiled to herself as she carried the bowl back down to the first floor. Anya had listened to her opinion. And because of that, Merlin might not have to have an operation.

• 2 •

"**H**ere, kitty," Stella said. She put the bowl with the milk-soaked bread into Merlin's cage.

Merlin got up and put his nose in the bowl. He smelled one of the pieces of bread, but pulled back without eating any. He sat down and began licking his belly.

Stella wasn't surprised Merlin wasn't eating. Marisa spoiled her pets. Merlin had probably spent the last three days feasting on table scraps. Stella figured he'd eat the bread once he got hungry.

"Stella! Muffin, come on, we're late!"

Stella jumped at the sound of her mother's

voice. She rushed toward Anya's office to get her coat. Her family was going horseback riding that morning and she did not want to be late.

The ride was a Christmas present from Stella's sister, Cora. Cora was fourteen. She worked at Jake's Stables after school. She loved going to the stables because she loved horses. Her favorite part of her job was taking tourists on rides in Goldenrock, the national park that surrounded their hometown of Gateway, Montana.

Jake, who had curly brown hair and a big bushy beard, was standing outside when Stella and her parents arrived at the stables. He was talking to a man, a woman, and two girls.

"Hello!" Jake greeted the Sullivans heartily. "Cora will be along in a minute. She's saddling up the last few horses. Let me introduce you to Mr. and Mrs. Armstrong and their daughters, Tiffany and Elaine. The Armstrongs are going on the tour with us today."

"Hi," Stella said. She smiled when she realized all four Armstrongs were wearing red baseball caps with white Cs sewn on them.

"Bob Armstrong!" Mr. Armstrong grinned as he patted his own chest and shook Norma's hand, then Jack's, then Stella's. "Family's out here on vacation. Live in Cincinnati, we do. Cincinnati—

with three *N*s and one *T*. Hate to see people misspell my hometown. I'm in the toothpaste business. Everyone needs toothpaste, right?"

Stella nodded, and so did her parents.

"Pleased to meet you," Mrs. Armstrong said quietly. "Where are you folks from?"

"We live just down the road," Norma explained. "Our daughter Cora works at the stables."

Elaine, the younger Armstrong girl, turned her pale blue eyes on Stella. She was about nine or ten.

"You are *so* lucky," Elaine whispered. "We've been in Montana for exactly twenty hours and I've already seen more animals than I saw in my whole life in Ohio. Do you like animals?"

Stella laughed and nodded. "I'm going to be a veterinarian when I grow up."

Elaine stared at her with admiration. "What a terrific idea," she said, as if she'd just decided to become a veterinarian, too. "Do you think we'll see any wolves during our ride?"

"I doubt it," Stella said. "The Goldenrock wolves have formed two packs and their territories are miles from here. Why—do you like wolves?"

Elaine nodded eagerly. "My bedroom is plastered with posters of them. That's why we came here on vacation—to see wolves."

Stella felt her chest puff out with pride. Her

family had fought for years to make sure a group of gray wolves were set free in Goldenrock. The battle had started before she was born.

"Have you ever seen a wolf?" Elaine asked.

Stella nodded. "My mom is a ranger in the park so I've seen them lots of times. She could tell you where to go to hear the wolves howl at night. It's really neat."

"I have to do that!" Elaine exclaimed. "Come on! Let's go ask her."

Elaine and Stella went over to the grown-ups. Norma gave Mrs. Armstrong directions to the wolf howl. The whole family seemed excited to go.

While they were chatting, Cora led out the rest of the horses.

"That's my sister," Stella told Elaine proudly.

Cora and Stella didn't look much like sisters. Stella had coppery red hair like Norma and Anya. Cora looked more like the girls' father. She had straight dark hair and a wide mouth.

Stella could tell that Cora was nervous about taking her family on a ride. Her cheeks were flushed and she kept petting Cinnamon, her favorite horse.

"Let's go!" Jake called out cheerfully. He helped everyone mount. Tiffany and Elaine slid gracefully into their saddles. Stella could tell they'd taken riding lessons. Mr. and Mrs. Armstrong were shaky, but Jake put them on gentle old mares. Stella was riding a frisky chestnut mare named Bay.

Cora and Cinnamon led the group across a field toward the park. The horses walked in single file. Elaine was in front of Stella and Mrs. Armstrong was behind her.

From the saddle, Stella could see Elaine's brown ponytail sticking out of the back of her baseball cap, the swishing tail of Elaine's horse, and Bay's head and pointed ears.

Everyone was quiet, enjoying the scenery. The only sound was the horses' hooves crunching through the crusty snow.

The sky was steely gray, and it had begun to snow. Stella caught one of the snowflakes on her mitten. The snowflake was long and skinny with sharp spikes.

"Look—reindeer!" Tiffany called. She was up ahead of Elaine, riding just behind Cora.

Elaine gasped.

Reindeer? Stella thought. The only reindeer in Montana were the plastic kind people put on their front lawns.

Stella followed Tiffany's outstretched finger with her eyes. Tiffany was pointing to a small group of elk. The elk had enormous branched racks. They actually did look like reindeer.

"Whoa, doggie!" Mr. Armstrong called. "I want to try out my new Christmas present. Folks back home won't believe this unless they have proof!"

Cora pulled on her reins, and the whole procession slowed to a stop. Mr. Armstrong took a shiny, professional-looking camera out of its case and clicked several photographs of the elk.

Elaine turned around in her saddle. "Real reindeer!" she said to Stella.

Stella smiled. "Actually, they're elk."

"Elk! Oh." Elaine didn't look the least bit disappointed.

Cora led the way across a deserted road and down a riding trail where the trees arched over their heads. A few minutes later, Cora led them out of the trees and into another pasture. Goldenrock started on the other side of the field.

"Look—buffalo!" Elaine shouted, sounding half amazed and half afraid.

Stella spotted six buffalo near a line of trees, about a football field away. Their enormous heads were lowered and they were using their noses to push aside the shallow snow.

"Stop! Stop!" Mr. Armstrong yelled. "I got to get a picture of this!"

Cora pulled up, and the group formed a rough bunch. Mr. Armstrong was fiddling with his camera.

"The buffalo that live in Goldenrock are very precious," Norma told the group. "They're the last remaining descedents of the enormous herd that once roamed the entire western Plains. Part of America's heritage."

"I thought the early settlers killed off all the buffalo," Mrs. Armstrong said.

"Nearly all," Norma told her. "A hundred years ago when Goldenrock began rebuilding the herd, fewer than fifty wild buffalo remained. It was sad because buffalo were at the center of the culture of the plains Indian tribes. Today, the park's herd is more than a thousand animals. Spiritually, the animals are very important to the area's remaining Native American population."

"So cool," Elaine muttered.

"What are they doing here?" Cora asked. "I've never seen them in this valley before."

"Must be the cold weather," Norma said. "That, and all the early snow we've had. The buffalo are traveling in search of food."

"This zoom lens is fantastic!" Mr. Armstrong said as he clicked off half a dozen photographs. "I can see the blades of grass in their mouths! Hey, I don't mind telling you these buffalo could use a powerful whitener. Are those teeth ever yellow!"

While the group was waiting for Mr. Armstrong to finish, a truck pulled into the center of the field. At first Stella thought it was the rancher who owned the property, but then she noticed that the truck had some sort of seal painted on one side.

"Who's that?" Stella asked her mom.

Norma shrugged. Cora urged her horse forward, and they began to move again.

Stella looked over her shoulder as her horse stepped forward. Two people—a man and a woman—had hopped off the truck. They were wearing green overalls, a lot like the park service uniform Norma wore.

They can't be park rangers, Stella told herself. *This is private land.*

The woman had a rifle in her hand.

"HoooHA!" The man shouted suddenly and ran forward.

"HAhaHA!" the woman yelled.

"What are they doing?" Stella called to Norma.

Norma was turning sideways in her saddle, watching the two figures in the center of the pasture. "Trying to drive the buffalo back into the park," she called.

"It's not working!" Stella called.

Only two of the buffalo had moved toward the line of trees that marked the park boundary. Four others had panicked and run back toward the road.

The woman ran after them for about twenty yards. Then she dropped to one knee and aimed her rifle.

"No way," Stella whispered.

BAM!

Stella's horse shuddered.

BAM, BAM, BAM!

The closest buffalo went down. First on his knees, then over on to his side. Stella blinked—and when she opened her eyes all four buffalo had crashed into the snow.

Stella swung her right leg over Bay's rump, resting her foot in the stirrup. She jumped off the horse's back, stumbling and half falling in the snow.

She got up, and began running, lurching toward the buffalo. Everything seemed far away. Her parents were yelling at her, but she couldn't make out their words. There was a hum in her ears like a motor engine idling.

• 3 •

Stella stumbled on through the snow. One of the buffalo was close enough so that she could see his mighty brown side heaving up and down. He was still alive, still breathing.

Stella was running forward, and then—

FWOMP! She was facedown in the snow. Jack was hugging her legs. He'd tackled her from behind.

"Let me go!" Stella demanded, wiggling to get loose. "I have to help the buffalo."

"No, it's too dangerous," Jack said. "Let your mother go."

Stella lay on her belly, watching her mother rush past. The officials met her halfway, blocking her from the animals. Stella could hear her mother's voice—high, hysterical, angry—but she couldn't make out her words.

Jack loosened his hold and he and Stella both got to their feet. "I want you to go back to the horses," Jack said.

"Where—are you going?" Stella was still breathless from being knocked down.

"To help your mom," Jack said.

"I want to come, too," Stella said fiercely. "She might need my help with the buffalo."

Jack hesitated and then nodded. They joined hands and strode together toward Norma. The four buffalo were lying still. Stella could see their bright blood against the snow.

"I told you—we work for the Department of Livestock," the man was insisting when Stella got close enough to hear. He had a blond mustache and a green ski cap.

"We don't have to take orders from you," the woman said angrily. "Any animals that wander out of Goldenrock are ours to deal with. If you want to keep them from getting shot, you should keep them on park land."

Norma took a deep breath. Stella could tell her mother was tense. Her back and shoulders were rigid.

"Let's not get into a turf war," Norma said. "Just explain to me—why would you *want* to shoot buffalo?"

"To stop the spread of brucellosis to cattle," the other woman said in a superior huff.

"Brucellosis!" Norma yelled. "The risk is zilch! There's never been a documented case of transmission from buffalo to cows. And cattle won't even be on this pasture for more than three months!"

"We have our orders!" the woman shouted.

"Mom," Stella said quietly. "Can we help them?"

"I'm afraid I can't let you examine the buffalo," the man said firmly. As if to underscore his point, he picked up the rifle he'd been resting on his boot.

Norma stared at the rifle for a moment that stretched on and on. "Let's go," she said quietly. She began to march toward the horses. Jack followed, dragging Stella along with him.

Stella's strength left her and she began to sob. She realized now that the buffalo would die. She kept hearing the bam of the rifle, seeing them collapse in the snow. She felt numb.

"What happened?" Cora demanded when they got close enough to hear her. "Who are those people?"

"They're from the Department of Livestock," Norma explained. "A state agency that protects cattle and sheep. They don't care about wild animals."

"Are the buffalo dead?" Elaine asked. Her eyes were red with tears.

"I got it all on film!" Mr. Armstrong said grimly.

"Let's take that film into town," Jack said. "I'm sure the national news wire services will be interested."

Everyone got onto their horses, and the group turned back toward the stables.

Stella kept her eyes straight ahead, the way Cora had taught her to ride years earlier, the horse's ears forming a V in front of her. She didn't want to look toward the field. She didn't want to see the motionless buffalo.

She felt ashamed Elaine and her family had witnessed such a terrible thing. This is what they would remember of Montana—this brutal murder.

The afternoon passed in a fog. Cora and Jake had to stay at the stables. Norma went into her office to report what had happened to the buffalo to the park rangers who managed the herd. Stella headed into town with her father and the Armstrongs. They dropped Mr. Armstrong's photographs off at the newspaper.

After dinner, the phone rang, and Stella talked to a reporter from the Associated Press. That night she dreamt that she and Elaine were loading buffalo onto an airplane so they could go live happily ever after in Cincinnati.

The next morning, Papa Pete arrived to pick up Stella before she had even finished her breakfast. Norma and Cora were still upstairs in bed. Papa Pete sat at the kitchen table and grunted when he saw the photograph of the downed buffalo in the morning paper.

"Awful, isn't it?" Jack said.

"Ranchers have always run things around here," Papa Pete said with a shrug. "I reckon they'll keep on running things for a while yet."

Stella stared at her grandfather. Why couldn't he just admit that it was awful? Maybe because he was a hunter. Papa Pete's job was leading tourists on big game hunts—for elk, bear, mountain lions. Maybe he couldn't admit that killing animals was ever wrong.

"So who's your friend?" Jack asked as he poured Papa Pete a cup of coffee.

"Widow by the name of Mrs. Hibbard," Papa Pete said. "Just moved out from Kansas. Always wanted a little sheep operation. Guess this is her idea of retirement."

"Chewy will be a big help to her," Stella said.

Papa Pete blew on his coffee and made a face. "Three-legged dog sounds like more trouble than help," he said. "But she wants him."

Stella was burning with fury, but she knew better than to talk back to Papa Pete. That would only make things worse. Still, it wasn't even nine o'clock and she was already grumpy.

"I'm ready," Stella announced, putting down her spoon. The sooner they left, the sooner she would be finished with Papa Pete.

Jack gave Stella a kiss good-bye. She put on her jacket, mittens, scarf, and hat and followed Papa Pete outside. They climbed into his big black truck and drove into town.

Anya had Chewy waiting in a dog carrier she was lending them. They put the carrier in the backseat and headed out toward Mrs. Hibbard's sheep farm.

Stella stared out of the side window, watching the ranches slide by. You could tell one family's property from the next because the style of fencing changed.

"It's starting to snow," Stella announced. This time the flakes that hit the windshield were fat and heavy—like clumps of white cotton.

Papa Pete switched on the windshield wipers. "It's really coming down," he said.

The snow accumulated quickly, covering the dirty brown snow on the side of the road with a clean white layer. The windshield wipers created a thick, wet pile of slush at the bottom of the windshield. Soon the snow began to stick on the road surface.

By the time Papa Pete turned off the County Road into Mrs. Hibbard's driveway half an hour later, about two inches of the white stuff had piled up.

Mrs. Hibbard was waiting for them outside her beautiful old stone barn. She was wearing a long red skirt with a purple jacket and work boots underneath. Her hair was silvery white and pulled into an enormous poofy bun.

"Oh, Peter," she said. "I'm so glad you're here. The radio says a blizzard is coming!"

Papa Pete grinned. "Well, I don't know if I can do much about that."

Mrs. Hibbard gave him a tolerant smile. "It's the sheep that have me worried. I drove them into the barn as soon as I heard the weather report. But a ewe and two lambs are missing."

"You sure?" Papa Pete asked.

"Peter, I only have twenty sheep," Mrs. Hibbard said. "I think I can count that high!"

Stella came around the side of the truck. Now

that she was outside, it seemed as if the snow was falling even more quickly.

"This is my youngest granddaughter, Stella," Papa Pete said formally. "Stella, Mrs. Roseanne Hibbard."

"Pleased to make your acquaintance," Mrs. Hibbard said distractedly.

"Don't worry, Mrs. Hibbard," Stella said. "I'll help you find your sheep."

Papa Pete looked up at the swirling snow. "I'm not sure that now is the best time for a treasure hunt."

"The snow is only going to get deeper," Stella said hotly.

Papa Pete was looking at Mrs. Hibbard. "Rose, listen," he said. "Shepherds are always losing sheep in sudden snowstorms. It's part of life. It would be best if you learned to accept it."

Mrs. Hibbard's face paled. She looked at Papa Pete in much the same way Stella imagined she looked at him herself. "Peter, I can't just let them die without trying to save them. These animals are my responsibility, my livelihood."

Papa Pete got a stubborn look on his face. "I didn't drive out here in a storm to go on some sort of wild goose chase."

No, Stella thought. *We came out here to deliver Chewy.* "What about Chewy?" she suggested. "He might be able to sniff out the missing sheep."

Papa Pete raised his eyebrows. "I doubt his nose is that good. Following scent in the cold and snow is difficult. Especially for a three-legged dog."

"I don't see the harm in trying," Mrs. Hibbard said.

Papa Pete was grumbling, but he opened the truck door and took out the carrier.

"Should I put him on his leash?" Stella asked.

"You don't leash farm animals," Papa Pete said gruffly. "Just let him go."

Stella opened the carrier's door and Chewy nosed his way out. He made his way around the barnyard, sniffing Stella's boots, then Papa Pete's, then Mrs. Hibbard's.

Mrs. Hibbard watched him. "Well, he seems to get around okay," she said doubtfully.

"Where were the sheep?" Stella asked.

"In the near pasture," Mrs. Hibbard. "It's only five acres. I don't see how they could have disappeared. Do you think they got out somehow?"

"You've got holes in your fence?" Papa Pete asked.

"No, no," Mrs. Hibbard said. "It's an old stone fence like the one near the barn. Quite sturdy."

Stella led the way into the pasture. Mrs. Hibbard followed eagerly, Papa Pete reluctantly. The snow was blowing harder than ever.

Chewy ran ahead, nose to the ground. His three-legged lope made him look dangerously off balance. He darted off in odd directions, occasionally running back to Stella.

"This dog is a pet!" Papa Pete said. "He's playing."

"Give him time!" Mrs. Hibbard said, scowling.

Stella didn't say anything. She knew Papa Pete was a dog expert. His hounds were some of the best in the county. She'd seen them track and tree a lion.

Chewy continued his zigzag path. He stopped near the fence only a few yards from Stella, and began to dig in the snow.

"No, Chewy," Stella said.

"Wait," Papa Pete said sharply.

The three of them huddled around Chewy.

The wind was blowing snow up against the fence, filling in the corner where the stone met the ground. The snowdrift was already two or three feet deep, and that was where Chewy was digging. He needed two legs to balance on, so he was digging with only one front leg. He wasn't making much progress.

"Rose, you got a shovel?" Papa Pete demanded.

"Sure, in the barn," Mrs. Hibbard said.

"I'll go," Stella offered. She ran through the snow and let herself into the dim barn where the other sheep were huddled together in one big enclosure. They were Merinos, medium-sized white sheep with fine, delicate fleece. Stella found a shovel to the right of the door and ran back into the field with it.

Papa Pete was just hauling a white lamb out of the snowdrift and handing him to Mrs. Hibbard. Mrs. Hibbard took a step back, struggling with the lamb's weight. Stella ran over with the shovel, and Papa Pete used it to uncover the lamb's mother.

"Wonderful, wonderful," Mrs. Hibbard said. "What a wonderful dog! I can't believe someone gave me this heroic dog for nothing!"

"Let's get these two into the barn," Papa Pete said.

"What about the other lamb?" Stella said.

"One thing at a time," Papa Pete said crossly.

He and Mrs. Hibbard began fighting their way toward the barn, leaning into the wind and blowing snow. Stella trudged along beside them, feeling the snow sting her face. Inside her mittens, her fingers were numb from the cold.

Stella pulled open the barn door. Mrs. Hibbard stumbled in, carrying the lamb. Then Papa Pete came in with the ewe. He immediately set her down, then slowly straightened up and rubbed his back.

Chewy trotted over to the sheep enclosure and lay down in front of it like a guard dog. He began gnawing chunks of ice out of his paws.

Stella and Mrs. Hibbard knelt to examine the sheep.

"They look okay to me," Stella said thoughtfully. "No frostbite on their ears or tails. They're not shivering. They don't seem to be in shock. . . ."

Stella let her voice trail off as she tried to think of what else she should check. Things were quiet in the barn and Stella could hear the wind howling outside. She felt a strange thrill. This was quite a storm!

"What wonderful creatures!" Mrs. Hibbard exclaimed. "So hearty. Buried in snow and no ill effects. And this dog! And this girl! Both quite useful. Peter, I don't know how to thank you."

"I wouldn't say no to a cup of coffee," Papa Pete said.

"Coffee? I can do better than that!" Mrs. Hibbard said. "I've got homemade soup and sandwiches on homemade bread. You've got to taste my sheep's milk cheese so you can tell all your friends how delicious it is!"

Stella studied the adults with sudden interest. All of the anger and worry had gone out of their voices. They sounded playful and happy, like Cora sounded when Joe Cummingham, a boy from her class, called. Could Papa Pete like Mrs. Hibbard as a girlfriend? *No way,* Stella told herself. *They're much too old for that.*

"Do you like pea soup?" Mrs. Hibbard asked Stella.

"Sure," Stella said. "But we can't have lunch yet. We're still missing a lamb."

"Oh," Mrs. Hibbard said. "Well, one lamb."

Stella stared right at her. Was she saying one lamb wasn't important?

"It's time for us to get in out of this storm," Papa Pete said.

"I'm not afraid of a little snow!" Stella exclaimed.

"That proves you're a foolish little girl," Papa Pete said. "A storm like this could be deadly, and human life is more important than any lamb."

Stella felt as if Papa Pete had slapped her. How

could he call her foolish? She'd just helped them save two of Mrs. Hibbard's sheep.

"Come inside, Stella," Mrs. Hibbard said in a gentler tone. "We need to get acquainted. And I'll show you my spinning wheel."

Stella allowed Mrs. Hibbard to lead her into the house. The house was cozy and welcoming. A big stone fireplace took up one whole wall. A fire was crackling in the grate. Mrs. Hibbard's spinning wheel was set up on one side. A wooden table big enough for twelve stood in the middle of the room. Three places were set at one end.

"Sit down, sit down," Mrs. Hibbard encouraged them after they'd peeled off their outdoor clothes and hung them up. "Let me put a flame under the soup. Stella, would you like a cup of hot chocolate?"

"Um, sure." Stella *was* cold.

Papa Pete sat down in an armchair near the fire. He stretched out his feet to warm them.

Stella didn't want to be near him. She went to the window and looked out. The swirling snow stopped her from seeing far. Somewhere out there was a lamb all alone.

"Why don't you both sit down at the table?" Mrs. Hibbard suggested.

They settled into their seats and the meal began. Stella answered Mrs. Hibbard's questions and ate a few spoonfuls of soup, but her mind was outside with the lamb. She wondered how he felt as the snow drifted up over his head. Could he breathe? Was he cold?

"More coffee?" Mrs. Hibbard asked Papa Pete.

Papa Pete put his hand over the cup. "We should think about getting on the road," he said. "Weather is only going to get worse."

"Maybe you should think about staying until the storm blows over," Mrs. Hibbard said. "I hate to think about you getting stuck on the road."

"Can't do it," Papa Pete said. "Got to feed my dogs, answer the phone. I have a business to run."

"At least stay for a piece of pie," Mrs. Hibbard said. "Peach. I made it this morning."

"Well, I guess another ten minutes won't matter one way or the other," Papa Pete said.

"May I go say good-bye to Chewy?" Stella asked.

"Don't you want any pie?" Mrs. Hibbard asked.

"No, thanks," Stella said. "I'm not very hungry."

"I don't want you going any farther than the barn," Papa Pete said.

Mrs. Hibbard shot him a sharp look. "Peter!"

"Don't worry, I won't," Stella said sullenly. She put on her outdoor clothes and let herself out in the snow.

The distance from house to barn was only

twenty feet, but even after that short walk Stella was happy to be out of the wind. Chewy lifted his head as she came in, then settled down again.

Stella knelt and petted his ears. She peered through the grate at the sheep. They were all lying down, piled together for warmth. All except for the ewe they had saved earlier. She was standing near the grate gazing out.

"Are you looking for your lamb?" Stella asked.

The ewe made no sign. She just stood gazing toward the door with her big black eyes.

Stella felt her anger rise up, swelling in her chest like a wet sponge. Anya or Norma would have helped her save the lost lamb. But not Papa Pete. He had called her a fool! *I'm not a fool,* Stella thought. *Papa Pete is just lazy and heartless.*

Chewy sighed. Somehow the sound helped Stella make up her mind.

"Come on, boy," she said. "Let's go find that lamb."

A minute later Stella and Chewy walked out into the stinging wind. Stella wasn't worried about Papa Pete seeing her from the house. The snow was blowing too hard for that.

Chewy seemed to know what Stella wanted. He led the way out into the near pasture, nose to the ground.

Stella didn't follow right away. She stared at the pasture, surprised by how much it had changed in the past hour. Along one side, only the very tip of the stone wall was still visible. At least another foot of snow had fallen.

Chewy was just a dark blob in the near distance. Stella shook herself and hurried after him. She didn't want the dog to get lost in the storm.

Five minutes, ten minutes passed. Stella trudged after Chewy as he made his weaving way around the pasture. Snow slipped into the top of her boots. She pulled her hat down to stop it from blowing off.

Finally Chewy stopped and began his one-legged digging. Stella hadn't remembered the shovel. She knelt down next to the furry dog and began to dig with her hands.

The snow was light and fluffy. They dug down a foot, two feet, three feet. Stella gasped when she caught sight of a tuft of curly fleece. An ear!

Stella and Chewy dug for another fifteen minutes. Then Stella worked her hands down into the snow and pulled. The lamb was much heavier than she expected. She was gasping by the time she wrestled him loose.

The lamb's eyes were half-closed. The tender skin inside his ear was blackened like a roasted marshmallow. That was frostbite—and it looked bad. But Stella could feel his heart beating strongly under her hands.

She stretched her arms around the lamb's legs and fought her way to her feet. The lamb's weight pushed her knee-deep into the snow.

Stella turned back toward the barn, anxious to get the lamb inside. Only . . . only . . . she couldn't see the barn. She turned slowly in a circle and saw nothing but blinding white flakes.

Stella was aware of her own breathing. She knew she was in danger, and yet felt strangely calm and detached. She thought, *If I die, Papa Pete will think I'm a fool for sure.*

She wanted to get back to the barn, and quickly, before Papa Pete tried to rescue her. But how? Stella remembered a story, maybe from one of the old *Little House on the Prairie* books, when a man wandered around in circles in the snow and almost died a few yards from his own front door. She couldn't just set out walking without a landmark to guide her.

Chewy sat looking up at Stella and whining.

Stella held the struggling lamb closer and tried to think.

Thinking about anything except the cold was hard. She could feel the wind against her eyeballs. The skin on her forehead felt numb. It was much colder than it had been that morning.

Stella felt a jab of fear. She didn't want to die in Mrs. Hibbard's near pasture. She wanted to be saved. She suddenly didn't care what Papa Pete thought.

"Help!" Stella hollered. "Help! Help!"

Yelling was useless. Stella could hardly hear her own voice over the raging storm. Nobody would hear her. Maybe it would have been better if she had left the lamb buried. At least buried in the snow, he was fairly warm and out of the wind.

I should bury him again, Stella thought. She imagined a cozy hole. *Maybe I should bury us all.* They could huddle together under the snow and keep each other warm.

Chewy paced around Stella in a circle.

"Chewy—dig!" Stella ordered.

The sheepdog gave one quick bark and began to run farther out into the field. "Chewy—no!" Stella shouted desperately.

Chewy stopped and sat back on his haunches. But when Stella approached, he dashed off again. Chewy wasn't wearing a leash. Stella's hands were full. She couldn't grab him.

"Bad dog!" Stella yelled as she stumbled after Chewy. Again, the dog sat down as if to wait for her.

Stella stopped walking. She was sure Chewy was leading her away from the barn. Following him was dangerous. Stella put the lamb down and started to dig a hole in the snow with her hands.

Chewy came bounding back. "Rraaa! Rraa!" he barked, nipping at the lamb's hooves.

The lamb ran forward, bleating.

"Chewy, stop!" Stella yelled.

But Chewy was still chasing the lamb, nipping at her hooves whenever she slowed down.

Stella ran after them, concentrating on keeping the animals within sight. She had no plan. Her only thought was to stop Chewy before he got too far out to pasture.

"Stella!"

She looked up, and was shocked to see the barn only a few feet ahead. Papa Pete was standing in front of the door with his hands on his hips. He looked angry. Stella took a deep breath to steady herself. She didn't want Papa Pete to see how frightened she'd been.

"Explain what you were doing in the pasture!" Papa Pete yelled.

Mrs. Hibbard lowered her eyes. She turned her attention to letting Chewy and the lamb into the barn. The animals rushed into the warm air.

"I went out to find the other lamb," Stella said, burning with injustice. Her parents never punished her in front of friends or out in public. Couldn't Papa Pete wait?

"You promised not to do that!" Papa Pete yelled.

"I know." Stella pushed by Papa Pete, making her own way into the barn. Mrs. Hibbard was kneeling in front of the lamb.

"Her ears are frostbitten," Stella reported. "Do you have any gauze and tape?"

"In the house," Mrs. Hibbard said.

"If you get them, I'll bandage the lamb's ears," Stella offered.

Mrs. Hibbard nodded without smiling. She got up and headed into the house.

"I'll give you five minutes to finish that and then we're leaving," Papa Pete said shortly.

Stella nodded. She moved around to examine the lamb's tail. She and Papa Pete were quiet the entire time Mrs. Hibbard was gone. When she came back, Stella awkwardly bandaged the lamb's ears.

"You should have my Aunt Anya look at this," Stella told Mrs. Hibbard. "She's the town veterinarian."

"Let's call her now," Mrs. Hibbard said.

"No," Papa Pete said. "Stella and I are leaving."

Mrs. Hibbard turned to him. "Now? The storm is getting worse!"

"Now," Papa Pete said.

"Foolish old man," Mrs. Hibbard said. "You're going to get yourself killed."

"No business of yours," Papa Pete said.

"You're no better than a child having a temper tantrum," Mrs. Hibbard said.

Papa Pete ignored her.

Stella kept quiet. She wanted to go, too. She wanted to get away from Papa Pete, to get somewhere she could breathe easier. She figured Papa Pete was probably just as eager to get away from her.

"Let's go," Papa Pete told Stella.

Stella hesitated, feeling bad for ruining the day. Not for Papa Pete so much, but for Mrs. Hibbard. "Thank you for lunch," she told Mrs. Hibbard. "And thanks for giving Chewy a home. He really is a great dog."

"I feel lucky to have him," Mrs. Hibbard said.

Stella dashed across the barnyard. She yanked open the door to Papa Pete's truck and climbed inside, relieved to be out of the howling wind.

A moment later Papa Pete climbed in the driver's side. He was silent as he started up the engine and backed out of the yard.

Stella relaxed a bit. He wasn't going to lecture her. That was a relief. But she couldn't relax for long. Papa Pete's disapproval hung in the air. Stella stared out the window and tried to think of something else.

The County Road was deserted. They passed a property with a split-wood fence half buried in snow. The wind came from Papa Pete's side of the road, pushing the truck sideways. His jaw was clenched and his eyes were narrowed with concentration as he fought to keep the truck on the road.

Stella couldn't see the sky. Everything was white—the snow, the clouds. The snowflakes swirled in front of the truck until Stella could hardly see the patch of snowy road lit up by Papa Pete's headlights.

"We'll stop under that bridge up there," Papa Pete said.

Stella nodded even though she couldn't make out the bridge. She felt satisfied. Papa Pete had been stubborn—just like she'd been—and he'd gotten them in trouble. Now they were going to have to sit in the truck until the worst of the storm blew over. He didn't even have a cell phone to call for help.

How could he make a big deal about her going out in the storm when he'd done something just as bad?

Stella caught a sudden movement out of the corner of her eye. She turned toward the driver's window. Up ahead, an old-style mobile home stood near the road at the end of a long open pasture.

The wind howled and the corner of the mobile home tipped up. When the wind quieted, the mobile home fell back onto all four supports.

"Papa Pete—watch out!" Stella said.

"I see it," Papa Pete said grimly.

The wind picked up again. It pushed, pushed, pushed. This time the mobile home tipped up too far. Stella watched in horror as it flipped up on one side. She could hardly hear the crash over the howl of the wind.

Stella sat forward in her seat and stared at the mobile home. Were there people in there?

"Hang on!" Papa Pete yelled. He jerked the steering wheel sideways. Stella held onto her seat as the truck bounced over the mound of snow on the side of the road and climbed up into the pasture.

"What are you doing?" Stella asked meekly.

Papa Pete stopped the truck next to the over-turned mobile home. He threw the truck into PARK. "Wait here," he told Stella. After a moment he added, "And I mean it this time!"

Stella huddled down in her seat as Papa Pete hopped out of the truck. Through the windshield, she watched him approach the mobile home. He circled it, looking for a way in. Stella saw him pull himself up on the edge, crawl across the top, and drop in through a window.

The clock in the dashboard read 12:41.

Stella took a deep breath. *I'm not going to worry about Papa Pete for five minutes,* she told herself. It would take him at least that long to crawl through the mobile home and find anyone who might be inside. She wished she could do something to help. How did Papa Pete survive without a cell phone? If she had been with her parents or Anya, she could have called 911.

The clock read 12:42.

What will I do if Papa Pete gets hurt or never comes out? Stella wondered. She pushed the frightening thought out of her mind. She didn't need to worry about something that probably wouldn't happen.

Probably wouldn't.

12:43.

Stella wondered if she should get out of the truck and see if Papa Pete was okay. *No,* she thought. *Even if he was hurt, he'd kill me.*

12:44.

Stella closed her eyes and tried to think about something other than Papa Pete. But the wind howling outside the truck pushed all other thoughts out of her mind.

12:45.

Stella scanned the mobile home, looking for some sign of what was going on inside. She gasped when she saw Papa Pete's cap poke out of the window. He climbed out holding what looked like a red sweater.

A moment later, Papa Pete got back into the truck.

"Was anyone in there?" Stella asked.

"All I found was this worthless mutt," Papa Pete said. He dropped the red sweater on Stella's lap.

Stella gently unwrapped the sweater as Papa Pete threw the truck into gear. Inside was a wiggling miniature dachshund. He wasn't much bigger than Rufus, although he was *longer*. The dog turned his black eyes on Stella and began to bark.

"Yip! Yip, yip, yip! Yip, yip, yip! Yip, yip, yip!" For such a little dog, he made a lot of noise.

"Can't you shut him up?" Papa Pete demanded. He pulled the truck back onto the road with a lurch.

"Shhh," Stella soothed the dog. She put him down on her lap but he wiggled off onto the seat.

"Yip, yip, yip!"

"I can't drive with all that noise," Papa Pete said.

Stella grabbed the dog and held his face. "Shush!" she said firmly.

"Yip, yip, yip!"

"Stella!"

"I'm trying," Stella said. "Maybe he's hurt!" She grabbed the dog and held him down on her lap.

Stella shifted around so she could examine the dog from every angle. She couldn't see any blood on his chocolate-brown fur. Next she ran her hand lightly over the dog's legs. The front legs were fine. But when Stella ran her hand over one of his back legs, the dog's yipping rose in pitch and volume. She could feel a sharp bone through the fur.

"Yip, yip, yip!"

"Stella, I asked you to shut him up."

"I can't," Stella said shortly. "His leg is broken. How much longer before we get to town?"

"Twenty, thirty minutes," Papa Pete said. "I can hardly see the road."

"I wish you had a cell phone."

"Well, I don't."

Stella wrapped the sweater around the dog to keep him warm and hold him still. She willed the truck to go faster. She did her best to tune out the dog's agonized barking and Papa Pete's irritation, but her stomach was churning.

The miles inched by. They turned onto the

mostly deserted highway. Slowly, the dog stopped barking so fiercely. He didn't quit altogether, but now his barks were spaced out a bit.

After a few miles, they passed a truck crawling the other way. The woman inside waved. They'd passed her by before Stella thought of flagging the woman down and asking her if she had a phone.

Papa Pete glanced at the little dog. "He doesn't look so good."

Stella looked down. The white corners of the dog's eyes were streaked with red. His chest rose way up with each breath.

"I hope Anya is at the clinic when we get there," Stella said.

Papa Pete grunted, keeping his eyes on the road.

Main Street looked odd without a line of traffic pulled up to the traffic light. As they drove through the main intersection, Stella noticed that the library was closed. So was Clip 'n Curl. Only the parking lot of the diner, The Wooden Spoon, had cars in it.

Stella anxiously scanned the street in front of the clinic. Her heart sank when she didn't see Anya's green truck anywhere. The lights in the clinic were dark. No smoke rose out of Anya's chimney.

"Can you carry the dog in?" Stella asked Papa Pete. "I'm going to look for Anya."

Without waiting for a reply, Stella ran inside. Anya wasn't in the clinic. Her apartment upstairs was dark and quiet. Stella rushed into the office. Boris, Anya's old basset hound, lifted his head in greeting and then went back to his nap. A piece of lined notebook paper lay next to the phone.

S—
I hope all went well with Chewy and Papa Pete's friend. Out on calls. Be back after lunch.
—A

Papa Pete came in carrying the dog. "Where should I put him?" he asked.

"Exam One," Stella said.

Papa Pete raised an eyebrow.

"It's the first door on the left," Stella told him. She picked up the phone, ready to tell Anya to get home pronto. Stella was halfway through dialing the number before she realized she hadn't heard the dial tone. She pressed the disconnect button and released it. Nothing.

Stella's heart began to race. She ran into Exam One. "The phone isn't working!" she told Papa Pete. He was standing over the exam table, looking down at the dog.

Papa Pete shrugged. "The storm must have knocked out the power lines."

"Well, that's just great!" Stella snapped. "What am I supposed to do now? I can't reach Anya, and that dog needs her help!"

"I thought you were some sort of veterinarian in training," Papa Pete said. "Can't you do something for him?"

"You don't understand!" Stella said. "Nobody is here to help me."

"Then you'd better get to work," Papa Pete said.

Stella felt like shaking him. Didn't he understand she was scared? The dog looked much worse. He'd even stopped barking. He just lay on the exam table, panting heavily.

"He's not going to get better by himself," Papa Pete said shortly.

"I know that," Stella snapped. She walked up to the table and took a deep breath. She'd seen Anya examine hundreds of dogs. First she listened to their pulse.

Stella grabbed the dachshund's elbow. She could hear his heart beating—but just barely. The speed of the heartbeats didn't mean anything to her, but she knew the fact that his heart didn't sound stronger was a bad sign.

Dogs in pain often bite. Stella knew that Anya

usually put a muzzle on injured dogs. But she had carried the dachshund on her lap all the way into town. If he had wanted to bite her, he would have done it already.

Stella pushed up the dog's lip. His gums looked pale. Almost white.

"He's in shock," Stella said quietly. "And he has a broken leg."

"What do we do now?" Papa Pete asked.

Stella stared at him. She'd never helped an animal without Norma, Jack, Anya, or her best friend, Josie, nearby.

Having Papa Pete there was no help at all. The way he watched Stella so intently made it hard for her to think. He seemed to be measuring her, judging her, and finding her a disappointment.

"Well?" Papa Pete demanded.

All Stella could think about was getting out of there. "You watch the dog," she said. "I'm going for help."

• 7 •

Stella ran out of the clinic's front door and down the snow-covered steps. Almost without thinking, she headed toward The Wooden Spoon. Earlier, Stella had noticed that the diner was one of the only businesses open on Main Street.

The storm hadn't let up. Stella tucked her head down and walked the block between the clinic and the diner tilted forward against the wind. When she got there, her face and fingertips were numb. Inside, the diner seemed incredibly warm and inviting.

Mrs. Crouse was standing behind the counter pouring coffee for a couple of men. Stella knew Mrs. Crouse because of her cat, Missy, and her kids, Pete and Maggie.

"Why, look who the wind blew in!" Mrs. Crouse exclaimed. Then she examined Stella's face, dropped her voice and added, "Is everything okay? You look about ready to burst."

"I've got a dog with a broken leg at the clinic," Stella explained. "Anya is out somewhere. I tried to call her but our phone isn't working. Can I— May I use yours?"

Mrs. Crouse pursed her lips and shook her head slowly. "Ours is down, too. Maybe some of the folks here have a cell phone you could use."

Stella looked at the two men at the counter.

"Sorry," one said.

"Sorry," the other one echoed.

Stella looked out over the half-filled restaurant. She wondered who to ask. Most of the people looked like tourists. They had cameras and guidebooks and wore those little pouches that fit around your waist.

Hurry, Stella told herself. She took a deep breath and walked up to a couple sitting in her father's favorite booth.

"Excuse me," Stella said. "But do you have a cell phone I could use? It's an emergency."

"Sorry," the woman said. "We left ours at home."

"Could be a while before we see it again," her husband said glumly. "Road to Billings is closed."

Stella's eyes widened. "It is?"

"Yup," the man said. "Had an eight-car pileup. Didn't you hear about it?"

Stella shook her head slowly. She suddenly realized she hadn't talked to her parents since early that morning. What if one of them had been in that accident? Or Anya?

A slender woman sitting in the next booth turned around. "I'm sorry, but I couldn't help overhearing," she said. "I have a cell phone, and I don't mind if you use it."

"Thanks!" Stella said gratefully, hurrying over to the woman's booth.

The woman handed her a bright red phone. "You'll need to dial one and the local area code before the number," she told Stella.

"I thought that was only for long distance," Stella said.

The woman smiled. "Well, my phone thinks I'm still in California."

Stella hesitated. "Isn't this going to be awfully expensive?" she asked.

The woman waved her off. "Don't worry about it," she said. She had a thick book with her. She opened it and began to read.

Stella sat down on the edge of the bench seat and turned on the phone. She quickly punched in

Anya's number. Relief washed over her when the call connected.

"Hello!" Anya shouted over the static on the line.

"Anya—it's Stella! Where are you?"

"Are you with your mom?" Anya shouted.

"No! Why?"

"She said she might come rescue me," Anya yelled. "She was going to try to borrow a snowmobile from the park service."

Stella absorbed this for a moment. It sounded as if her mother was okay. At least that was good news. "Why does Mom need to rescue you?" Stella demanded. "Where are you?"

"Chico Hot Springs," Anya said. "The roads are a mess. Trees are down. Electrical lines, too. The road is closed until the plows come through. And that might not be until sometime tomorrow!"

Stella's chest tightened. Tomorrow . . . but she needed help *now*. "Anya, we've got a little dog in the clinic with a broken leg."

"I'm glad you're there!" Anya said. "Did you splint the leg?"

"Not yet," Stella admitted. "The dog is in shock, too."

"Okay, you'll need to start an IV," Anya said. "Getting in some saline solution will help his heart pump harder."

"I've never put in an IV!" Stella said.

"I'll talk you through it," Anya said.

"You can't!" Stella said. "I'm not at the clinic. I'm at The Wooden Spoon on a borrowed cell phone."

"Then take some notes," Anya said.

Stella borrowed a pen from the woman who'd lent her the phone. She took notes on a napkin, writing down Anya's instructions on how to find a vein, where to get the saline solution and lots of other details.

"Watch him carefully until I get there," Anya said after she had answered all of Stella's questions. "And check on Merlin."

Merlin! Stella had forgotten all about Marisa's cat!

"You'll do fine," Anya said.

"Thanks," Stella whispered. She turned off the phone and handed it back to the woman.

"You need to call anyone else?" the woman asked. "I don't mind."

Stella thought for a minute. Then she dialed her home number.

"Hello?"

"Daddy, it's Stella."

"Hi, Muffin, where are you?" Jack asked. "I've been worried about you!"

"I'm at The Wooden Spoon," Stella told him. She explained about the dachshund, Papa Pete, and the nice lady from California.

"Your mom is at work," Jack reported. "The park rangers are having an emergency meeting about the buffalo. I'm going to call her and tell her to get to the clinic as soon as possible."

"But Mom is supposed to go rescue Aunt Anya," Stella pointed out. "She's stuck on the side of the road in Chico Hot Springs. And what if a really big emergency comes along before she gets back?"

"First things first," Jack said.

Stella hated the idea of Anya being stranded. But she wanted her mother's help. "Okay, Daddy, thanks," she said. "How's Rufus?"

"Rufus is just fine," Jack said. "He's curled up in front of the fire."

"Is Cora there?"

"Yup," Jack said. "We're all safe and sound. Good luck with the dachshund."

"Thanks," Stella said.

"Bye, Muffin."

Stella turned off the phone. "This time I'm really finished," she told the woman from California. "Thanks."

"You're welcome," the woman said. "Good luck."

"Thanks." Stella grabbed the napkin with her notes and headed for the door.

She felt better. Anya had told her exactly what to do with the IV. She still wasn't crazy about the idea of putting a needle into the dog's vein. But Anya thought Stella could do it, and that gave Stella confidence. She was also glad her mother was coming to the clinic. She'd be able to fix any mistakes Stella made.

"Thanks, Mrs. Crouse," Stella called.

Mrs. Crouse looked up from the order she was taking and waved.

Stella went outside and ran down the street. This time the wind pushed her along. She let herself into the darkened clinic. "Papa Pete, I'm back!" she hollered.

Papa Pete came out of Exam One. His expression was serious. "What took you so long?" he asked.

"I had to find a phone to use," Stella said. "And then Anya had to tell me what to do."

Papa Pete shook his head slowly. "Well, you're too late," he said gravely. "I think you've lost him."

Stella pushed by Papa Pete and ran into Exam One.

The little dachshund was still on the exam table. He was stretched out on his side, panting and shivering. His eyes were open but unfocused.

Stella pushed up his lip and saw that his gums were even paler than they'd been earlier. She grabbed his elbow but had to concentrate hard before she could feel his pulse.

Papa Pete was standing in the doorway. He was frowning disapprovingly, as if he blamed Stella for the dog's state. He watched as Stella pulled off her coat and hat, washed her hands and crossed back to the dog.

Stella opened a drawer under the table. She pulled out an IV set—a needle with a short length of tube attached.

Next she got out a foot-long length of rubber. Stella tied the rubber six inches down from the hip joint of the dachshund's good front leg. After a moment she saw a vein pop up near his elbow.

Stella's hands were sweating. The next part was hard: She had to slide the needle into the vein without inserting it too far.

"Am I supposed to shave off the fur over the vein?" Stella wondered aloud. Anya hadn't mentioned that.

Stella glanced at Papa Pete. He didn't offer any advice.

"I'm going to skip that," Stella told herself. "Dachshunds don't have much fur. At least, not smooth dachshunds. Things might be different if this little guy was a long-hair."

Stella's hands were shaking as she took the needle out of its sterile wrappings. She took a deep breath and positioned herself over the dachshund's leg. She moved the needle toward the bulging vein. But she couldn't make herself slide it in.

"You need help?" Papa Pete asked gruffly.

"No." Stella gritted her teeth and gently pushed

the needle in. She stopped when she saw the tip puncture the vein.

Anya had told Stella how to make certain the needle was properly placed. She had to open the syringe a tiny bit. Stella tried it. The syringe's receptacle filled with blood. That was a good sign.

Stella unclipped the syringe, leaving the needle in place. She went to a cabinet and found a bag of saline solution. She unwrapped the bag and put it on an IV stand.

Now all she had to do was connect a tube attached to the bag with the one attached to the needle and open a valve so the saline would start dripping. When she finished, Stella let out all her breath in a rush. She felt as if she'd been holding it for hours.

"Now I just have to splint his leg," Stella said.

This part didn't scare her. She'd put a splint on a deer's leg once. That time, she'd been out in the woods and struggling with a wild animal. Splinting the dachshund was easier because the clinic had all of the supplies she needed.

Stella laid two short aluminum rods along the dog's leg. She secured them with gauze and tape. When she finished, she checked the dog's pulse. The movement under Stella's fingers was definitely stronger. Stella pulled a chair up to the exam table and sat down. She was tired.

Papa Pete was still standing in the door. "Where's Anya?"

"Trapped by the storm," Stella reported. "But Mom should be here soon."

"I'm going upstairs to make some coffee," Papa Pete said.

"Fine."

Stella was happy to be alone. Exam One was peaceful. Stella stroked one of the dog's good legs and waited for her mom to come. She was looking forward to showing Norma what she had done.

And the kids at school! Stella would have a great time telling Josie and Marisa this story.

Suddenly Stella sat upright.

Marisa!

She'd forgotten all about Merlin.

Stella jumped up and rushed back to the boarder room.

She expected Merlin to peek out at her as she came in. He didn't. In the half light, Stella couldn't see anything but the regular grid of the cage front. She flicked on the light and stepped quickly toward the cage. Stella gasped when she got close enough to see inside.

Merlin was lying on the bottom.

"Here kitty, kitty, kitty," Stella choked out.

He didn't move.

"Oh no, oh no, oh no," Stella said while she opened the cage door, pulled the cat out, and checked his pulse. It was weak. Very weak.

Stella could guess what happened. The tinsel had sliced through Merlin's bowel. Now his digestive juices were poisoning him.

Stella remembered her promise to Marisa. Marisa would never forgive her if Merlin died. "Please don't die," Stella whispered to the cat.

But that was stupid. She couldn't just stand there hoping everything turned out okay. She had to act.

Stella carefully put Merlin back in his cage, then ran into the operating room and got her coat. She decided to go back to The Wooden Spoon. If Merlin was going to live, she was going to need Anya's help. Stella just hoped the nice woman from California would still be in the diner.

"Papa Pete!" Stella hollered up the stairs.

He didn't answer right away. In that quiet moment, Stella heard a sound like a low rumbling. It sounded like the garbage truck. They wouldn't be collecting garbage during a snowstorm, would they? Suddenly Stella knew what it was. Her mother's snowmobile!

Stella ran toward the back door and threw it open.

Norma had driven the glistening black machine right into Anya's backyard and parked it near the flight cage. "Hi, Muffin," she said as she pulled off her helmet and shook her hair loose.

"Mom," Stella said breathlessly. "I think Marisa's cat is dying."

"Where is he?" Norma asked.

"In the boarder room."

"Where's your grandfather?"

"Upstairs making coffee."

Norma jogged up the steps. She pulled her cell phone out and tossed it to Stella. Then she continued on inside and bent to examine the cat.

Stella dialed quickly. When Anya picked up, she described the situation in a few short sentences.

"Tell your mom to knead Merlin's stomach," Anya said.

Stella told Norma.

"It feels hard," Norma reported.

"It's hard," Stella said. "What does that mean?"

"It means Merlin needs emergency surgery to repair his bowel," Anya said. "You and Norma will have to do it."

"We have to operate," Stella told her mom.

Norma laughed and shook her head. "I don't

know," she said uncomfortably. "Talk to me about wolves and bears and bats, and I'm fine," she said. "But surgery isn't something I do very often. And cats aren't exactly my specialty."

"Mom says—"

"I can imagine," Anya interrupted her. "Listen, Stella, you're going to have to assist your mother. Encourage her and point out any problems you spot."

"We definitely have to do this?" Norma demanded.

"Merlin will die if you don't," Anya said.

Stella nodded at her mother.

"Let's get him into the operating room," Norma said.

For the next twenty minutes, Norma and Stella did what Anya told them to do over the phone.

They changed into scrubs, washed their hands, and put on gloves. Norma inserted Merlin's IV—it took her only about ten seconds! Stella helped Norma find the medicine that would put Merlin to sleep. Anya told them how to calculate the correct amount based on the cat's weight.

After Merlin was asleep, Norma and Stella tied the cat to the table. They shaved Merlin's belly and covered it with antiseptic. Stella gathered scalpels, tweezers, and sutures. She turned on the bright operating lights.

"I guess we're ready to go," Norma said. She didn't sound exactly thrilled.

"Tell your mom to mark the midpoint of Merlin's belly," Anya told Stella over the phone. "Then she should cut from there down to Merlin's pelvis. She's going to be exposing the bowel."

Stella relayed this message.

Norma picked up a scalpel. She took a deep breath. "Here goes nothing," she said. Norma touched the knife to Merlin's skin. Stella saw the first bead of blood.

Suddenly the lights above Norma's head went out! There was a low whine as all of the electrical machines shut off.

"What just happened?" Stella said. The operating room was so dark she couldn't see her hand in front of her face.

"The power went out," Norma said.

"What's going on?" Anya demanded over the static on the cell phone.

"Power's out," Stella told her. "What should we do now?"

"Hope it comes back on," Norma said.

"I have a backup generator," Anya said. "It should kick in. Give it a minute."

Stella stood staring up at the darkened lights. The ceiling creaked as Papa Pete moved around up in Anya's apartment. Stella could hear her own heart beating and a low crackling over the cell phone.

They waited.

Stella's mind raced.

What would happen to Merlin if the lights didn't come back on?

His surgery would definitely have to wait. But Anya had said he needed *emergency* surgery. Would waiting kill him?

Another thing worried Stella: Norma had already started to cut. What would happen to that open incision if they couldn't continue? They wouldn't be able to stitch it up in the dark.

And another thing: The machine that administered the medicine that kept Merlin asleep ran on electricity. Without it, Merlin would eventually wake up. Stella shuddered. Imagine waking up in the middle of surgery.

Stella jumped as the pump started to beep. There was a low whine, and then the lights came on.

Norma let out a huge sigh. "We're back in business," she said. She leaned forward, positioned the scalpel, and continued the incision. She had just finished when Papa Pete burst into the operating room.

"Hey, Norma," he said. "You ladies okay?"

Norma glanced up quickly. "Just fine."

"Crazy storm isn't finished with us yet," Papa Pete said. "I'm going downstairs, check the circuit breakers."

"Thanks," Norma said.

"Can you see the bowel yet?" Anya asked over the phone.

Stella peered into Merlin's open belly. "Mom, where's the bowel?" she asked.

"There." Norma gestured with her tweezers toward what looked like a mound of pink worms.

"Oh, gross," Stella said. The bowel reminded her of a clump of insect larva she'd once overturned digging in her parents' yard. Larva, bowel—they were both things best hidden from view.

"Sounds like you've got it," Anya said with a little laugh. "You should be able to identify the dead part by color. It will be gray from lack of normal blood flow."

"We're looking for a gray part," Stella told her mother.

Norma nodded absently. She was gently pushing the bowel aside, exposing different pieces to the light. Stella watched, too. "There!" she said.

"I see it," Norma said. A six-inch-long piece of bowel looked lifeless, like the ashes in the bottom of a glowing fire. "What do I do now?"

They worked intensely for over an hour. Norma snipped out the dead section of bowel. Part of the tinsel came out with it. Norma followed the tinsel back into a healthier part of the bowel, cutting out piece after tiny piece.

Stella relayed Anya's directions to her mother. Twice she held the tweezers while Norma worked delicately with the scissors. She checked Merlin's pulse.

"I think I got it all," Norma finally announced.

"Mom's got all of the tinsel," Stella told Anya.

"What?" Static practically drowned out Anya's voice.

"No more tinsel!" Stella hollered.

"Norma needs . . . loose ends . . .—el!" Anya shouted back. Stella could only hear about half of what Anya was saying. The rest was too faint or broken up by hissing, crackling, and pops on the line.

"I think you're supposed to attach the loose ends," Stella told her mother. "But it's really hard to hear Aunt Anya."

"Her battery must be dying," Norma said.

"Should I hang up?" Stella asked.

Norma nodded. "That's probably best. Let's save the rest of her battery in case we really need her."

"Aunt Anya!" Stella shouted into the phone. "We're going to hang up so we don't totally waste your battery."

"Goo . . . ck . . ."

Stella turned off the phone with a pang of misgiving. She'd felt more confident when Anya was there to walk them through each step of the operation.

"I hope Anya is okay all by herself," Stella said. "The sun must have gone down by now."

"She'll be fine," Norma said. "I'm going to go pick her up as soon as we're finished here."

Stella watched nervously as her mother used tiny stitches to connect the bowel.

"Being a vet is hard because you treat so many species," Norma said thoughtfully as she worked. "Doctors only have to deal with one species—

human beings. People are all more or less the same inside. But a dog isn't much like a horse or a bird."

"Or a snake or a ferret," Stella said, naming some of the other animals she'd seen in the clinic.

Norma clipped off one suture and started on another. "On the other hand, bowel is bowel. Not too much unique or exciting about the stuff."

Stella smiled, sensing that the worst was over. Her mother seemed more relaxed and in control. She felt her own shoulders relax half an inch.

"I wonder if Aunt Anya has any frozen pizza upstairs," Stella said. She was hungry. Was it dinnertime already? Stella was glancing at the clock when—

WAAAaaaaaa . . .

The lights clicked off. Darkness.

"Not again," Norma muttered angrily.

Stella turned her face up toward the lights. She blinked slowly, but there wasn't much difference between eyes open and eyes shut.

Anya had said it took the generator a minute to kick in. Stella counted silently to herself in the darkness. *One, one thousand, two, one thousand . . . sixty, one thousand.*

Nothing.

Stella heard Papa Pete clumping down the hallway. "Generator's out," he called as he passed the door of the operating room. "I'm going back down to the basement to see what I can do."

"How long will that take?" Stella wondered.

Norma sighed. "You best see if you can find a good flashlight," she said.

Stella knew where Anya kept one—on the shelf next to the back door. She rushed down the dark hallway, trailing one hand along the wall. When she got to the door, she stood on her tiptoes and felt along the shelf until her fingers brushed a solid object. Stella lifted the heavy flashlight and found the switch by touch.

The light clicked on and Stella felt grateful for Anya's preparedness. She ran back down the hall to the operating room.

"Shine it on the table," Norma said. "I want to close before the poor cat wakes up."

Stella held the light high overhead so it was shining onto Merlin's belly.

Norma began to sew up the incision. One stitch, then another, and another after that.

Stella's arm went numb. She switched the light to her left hand while she shook some blood into her right. Ever so slowly, Norma closed the incision.

"Do you need a break?" Norma asked.

"No," Stella said, ignoring her aching shoulders. "Go ahead and finish."

Norma removed the oxygen mask. She took the tube out of Merlin's throat and put a bandage over his incision.

"I think we're ready to move him," Norma said.

Stella held the light while her mother carried Merlin into the boarder room. Norma had just closed Merlin's cage when the lights came back on.

Norma and Stella exchanged looks.

"Perfect timing," Norma said.

Papa Pete came clumping up the stairs. "We're running on the generator," he reported. "I had to fix an oil leak. If we're lucky it should hold for the night. I'm walking down to the station for more gas."

"You're a lifesaver," Norma said.

Papa Pete just grunted and kept going. A moment later, Stella heard the door slam.

"Mom, could you check the little dog with a broken leg?" Stella said. "Make sure his IV is okay?" She was half afraid the lights would go out before Norma had a chance.

"Sure," Norma said.

They went down the hallway to Exam One together. The dachshund started a low whining bark when he saw them. "Arr, arr, arrrruuuuuuu," he moaned.

"What's the matter?" Stella demanded.

"Sounds like the little guy is in pain," Norma said.

"I haven't given him any medicine," Stella said. "He was out cold when you got here."

"Don't worry," Norma said. "We'll fix him up."

Stella approached the table. "Shh," she told the dog. She stroked him between the ears. "It's okay, everything is going to be okay."

Norma went to the cabinet and unlocked it. She took out a small tube of medicine and checked the dosage on the label. Then she went over to the dachshund and examined his IV.

"Looks good to me," she told Stella.

Stella felt her chest swell with pride. She'd done okay, all on her own. She watched as Norma drew the medicine into a syringe and injected it into the dachshund's thigh muscle.

"He'll feel much better in a few minutes," Norma predicted.

The dog stopped his howling whine, but he still looked miserable. His head was hanging and his eyes were sad.

"I want to stay with him until he calms down," Stella said.

"Good idea." Norma pulled up another chair and sat. Stella took the chair next to the examining table.

"How was the buffalo meeting?" Stella asked.

Norma pressed her lips together. Her cheeks flushed. "Very informative," Norma said angrily. "Apparently the Department of Livestock is rounding up buffalo that stray off park land."

"What do they do with them?" Stella asked.

"A retired rancher owns that property we were crossing with Jake," Norma said. "Apparently the Department of Livestock talked her into letting them set up a corral on her property."

"Why don't they just bring them back into the park?" Stella asked.

"They want to test them for a disease called brucellosis," Norma said. "If they test positive, they'll shoot them."

The dachshund was blinking his eyes sleepily. Stella rubbed his silky ears. She was remembering the sight of the buffalo crashing into the snow.

Norma shook her head slowly. She reached out and stroked one of the dog's feet. "I can't let this happen, and at the same time I can't do anything to stop it," she said sadly.

"We could just sneak in and let the buffalo go," Stella suggested, only half seriously.

Norma didn't smile. "I thought of that," she said. "But it's private property. If I got caught, I could get fired. That's too big of a risk to take."

Stella stared at her mom.

Norma hadn't said that setting the buffalo free was wrong. Only that she couldn't risk getting caught.

Stella didn't mind getting caught.

• 10 •

Stella saw Papa Pete come up the front steps. He knocked the snow off his boots and then opened the front door. A moment later he poked his head into Exam One. "Operation finished?" he asked.

Norma nodded and stood up slowly. "I was just heading out."

"Where are you going?" Papa Pete asked.

"I borrowed a snowmobile from the park service," Norma said. "I thought I'd pick up Anya before another emergency drops in our lap."

Papa Pete nodded.

"I don't want to leave Merlin and the dachshund," Stella said.

"That's okay," Norma agreed. "As long as Papa Pete doesn't mind hanging out until morning, I think it's best if you stay here."

"Road up to my place is probably impassable," Papa Pete said.

"We should be back before light," Norma said. "I'll leave you my cell phone so you're not so cut off from civilization."

"No," Papa Pete said. "You'll need the phone in case your snowmobile breaks down. Take it with you."

"Pete—" Norma started.

"Take it, Mommy," Stella said. "Please?"

"Oh, all right," Norma agreed. Ten minutes later, she left.

Stella checked on the animals one last time. Then she climbed up the stairs to Anya's apartment. There wasn't any pizza in the freezer. Papa Pete boiled up some hot dogs. Stella ate two on slices of rye bread with mustard and pickle relish.

After she finished eating, Stella took off her boots and jeans and slipped into Anya's bed. Papa Pete stretched out on the couch. It was early—earlier than Stella went to bed at home—but Stella didn't have anything to read and Papa Pete said they shouldn't use generator power for the TV.

Stella stared up at the ceiling. Before long, she

heard Papa Pete begin to snore. Stella couldn't sleep. She was imagining the buffalo locked inside a corral. Norma had told her that buffalo used to roam states like Montana in herds so big their hoofbeats sounded like distant thunder to the early settlers. Now people said the remaining buffalo had to stay within the borders of the park.

That wasn't fair.

Stella's mind turned to Marisa and Merlin. What would she say to Marisa if the cat died? Stella wished she hadn't opened her big mouth the day before. If she'd let Anya operate when she wanted to, Merlin would be okay by now.

Headlights lit up the ceiling. Stella heard a car pull up right in front of the clinic. She crawled out of bed and peeked out the window. At the same time, someone began pounding on the clinic's front door.

An emergency, Stella thought.

"What the—" Papa Pete bellowed from the living room. "All right, already! I'm coming, I'm coming. Keep your shirt on."

Stella heard her grandfather start down the stairs. She grabbed her pants and pulled them on. She laced up her boots as quickly as possible. The distraction was almost a relief. At least now she wouldn't have to sit in bed and worry about Merlin and the buffalo.

"Papa Pete?" Stella called as she pounded down the stairs. "What's happening?"

"Sick dog," Papa Pete called back. "Not the most unique circumstance in the county today. In fact, I've got to say the novelty is wearing off."

Stella could hear the disapproval in Papa Pete's voice. She expected to see a little dog like Rufus. Papa Pete had no use for little dogs. He thought they were useless. So Stella jumped when she came out into the waiting room and found herself eye-to-eye with a Great Dane.

Without meaning to, Stella took a step back. Big dogs didn't scare her. But this dog wasn't big—he was *huge*.

The Dane also seemed jittery. He paced to the end of his metal-link leash, sat down, got up, paced back to his owner, and then started the whole sequence over again.

Holding onto the heavy-duty leash was a man who stood only shoulder-high to Papa Pete. Stella guessed the man got a lot of jokes when he walked his dog in public. The Dane looked as if he could drag his owner wherever he wanted to go. The man looked frantic, wild. His eyes were red and swollen.

"Where's Anya?" the man demanded.

"Stuck in Chico Hot Springs," Stella said.

"Can we call her?" the man asked.

"The phone line is out," Stella reported.

"I told him all that already!" Papa Pete said irritably.

"I'm sorry, I'm sorry," the man said in a high-pitched cry. "I just can't believe she's not here in our hour of need! Anya has been like a mommy to Titus ever since he was a wee puppy. She even talked me out of getting his ears cropped."

"What's your name?" Stella asked. She'd just noticed that the man was holding a white plastic box in his leash-free hand. The box was almost exactly like the one Stella kept her crayons and colored pencils in at home.

"Chris—Chris For-ester," the man choked out. The man's bottom lip started quivering and he began to cry. Papa Pete hated it when Stella cried. She could imagine how he was going to react to *this*.

"Oh, for heaven's sake!" Papa Pete said. "Buck up! I didn't get out of bed to listen to you weep. Tell us what's wrong with your dog. Maybe we can do something to help."

"Can't you see?" Mr. Forester demanded. "Look at his belly!"

Stella looked.

Titus's belly did not look good at all. It was

sticking out so far Stella almost wondered if Titus had swallowed a balloon. Under the dog's short fur, Stella could see that his skin was shiny—like skin can get when it's swollen up. Titus was letting his enormous head droop down like it was too heavy to hold up. His platter-sized tongue hung loose out of one side.

Then Titus jerked his head forward in a powerful gag, and then another.

"Watch out," Stella said.

Papa Pete and Mr. Forester stepped back.

Stella braced herself for a liquid splash on the floor. She figured Titus had eaten some rotten food. Dogs did that all the time. He'd feel much better once he got it out of his system. But Titus continued to gag for several minutes. Nothing came up. Slowly the big dog relaxed.

"Poor baby!" Mr. Forester said. He leaned down slightly and put his arm around Titus's neck.

Stella was puzzled. "Has Titus eaten anything strange today?" she asked.

Mr. Forester seemed offended. "Why do you ask?"

"Maybe Titus has food poisoning," Stella said with a shrug.

Mr. Forester shook his head. "It's bloat. My breeder warned me that big dogs are susceptible to it. I wanted to be prepared, so I bought this off the Internet." He waved a white box around in the air.

"If you had your stupid kit, why didn't you take care of your dog at home?" Papa Pete demanded.

"I just . . . couldn't," Mr. Forester said.

Stella stepped forward and took the box. It said BLOAT KIT in red letters on the outside. In smaller type it read, NOT A SUBSTITUTE FOR VETERINARY CARE.

Mr. Forester buried his face in Titus's neck. "Hang in there, baby," he murmured.

Stella took the box over to the reception desk. Papa Pete came up behind her and looked over her shoulder.

"What's bloat?" Papa Pete whispered.

"I don't know," Stella whispered back. She wasn't too worried. Titus didn't seem terribly sick. And since he was already a patient of Anya's, Stella figured she could put him in the boarder room until Anya and Norma got back.

Stella opened the box. Inside was a stomach tube, some lubricant, a cheap stethoscope, three rolls of tape, and a very large and long needle. That needle gave Stella a bad feeling.

Tucked into the bottom of the box, Stella spotted several pieces of copy paper folded in half. She pulled out the paper and began to read.

Properly administered first aid will increase the chances a dog with bloat will survive once it gets to a veterinarian.

Stella raised her eyebrows. Survive? Increase the chances? That sounded pretty scary. Maybe bloat was more serious than she'd realized.

Please read all of these instructions and make sure you understand them before administering first aid. Stella groaned. Why did instructions always say that? She counted the pages. There were seven of them covered in teeny, tiny type with plenty of diagrams to study.

Stella's eyes skipped down the page.

BLOAT IS A LIFE-THREATENING EMERGENCY. Her eyes widened and she started to read more quickly.

Symptoms may include heavy salivating, whining, pacing, getting up and lying down, and unproductive attempts to vomit. Severe symptoms—such as a rapid heartbeat and a weak pulse—are normally followed by prostration and death.

Stella didn't know what "prostration" meant. But she understood "death" well enough.

"I think he's getting worse," Mr. Forester said fearfully.

Stella spun around. Titus was panting, drooling, and gagging all at once. He started a low whine that sounded like an eighteen-wheeler rumbling to life.

Somehow Stella didn't think she was going to have time to read all of the directions.

• 11 •

Help me," Stella said to Papa Pete. She turned the bloat instructions to page four and put them down on the reception desk.

"Why? What are you going to do?" Papa Pete asked.

"Help this dog before it's too late," Stella said. She'd skimmed through the first half of the directions and hadn't seen anything she couldn't handle. Actually, the written instructions made Stella feel confident. In most emergencies she had to rely on memory and guesswork.

Only one thing made Stella uncomfortable: She needed help. Mr. Forester obviously wasn't going to be much use. That left Papa Pete.

"Mr. Forester, you're going to have to get out of the way," Stella said.

"Okay, okay!" Mr. Forester scrambled back and settled into one of the waiting room chairs. He seemed glad that someone was taking charge.

"Could you please hold his head steady?" Stella said to her grandfather.

Papa Pete took the leash and held it tightly. His expression was blank. Stella guessed he didn't like taking orders from her. At least he wasn't lecturing her.

Stella ripped a long piece off one of the rolls of tape and stuck one end onto her shirt. Then she put one hand on Titus's lower jaw and forced his mouth open.

The dog didn't resist.

Stella noted that Titus's gums were pale—a sign of a weak heartbeat. She grabbed the roll of tape and slipped it between Titus's substantial teeth. She placed it so the hole in the center of the tape roll faced the front of the dog's mouth. She felt as if she were working on a lion or a dinosaur. If he decided to bite . . .

Don't think about that, Stella told herself. Titus needed her help and she couldn't help him if she was afraid of him.

Stella pulled the loose piece of tape off her shirt.

She quickly wrapped it around Titus's muzzle. That was to keep the roll of tape in place.

"Hand me that tube," Stella said to Papa Pete. He snatched it off the reception desk and gave it to her.

Stella aligned one end of the tube with the rib closest to Titus's tummy. Then she ran the tube along his side. Her movements were sure and practiced. Stella had used a stomach tube to feed Rufus for almost the first week she had him. This wasn't much different. In fact, it was easier because Titus wasn't as fragile as Rufus had been.

"Can you mark where the tube comes out of his mouth?" she asked Papa Pete.

Papa Pete grabbed a Magic Marker off the desk. He marked a neat line on the part of the tube just under Titus's black nose.

Stella reached out and grabbed the lubricant. She squeezed some onto one end of the tube and smeared it around. Stella gently threaded the tube through the hole in the tape roll. She felt some resistance when the tube hit the back of Titus's throat, but then Titus started to swallow and the tube slid in.

Papa Pete was watching intensely. Mr. Forester had buried his face in his hands.

Stella put her mouth to the end of the tube. She blew gently into the tube while guiding it in. Stella was focused on the mark on the tube. She knew it was important not to push the tube in too far. Enough pressure and the tube could go straight through the wall of Titus's stomach.

Stella had another reason to watch carefully. The bloat first aid directions said when the tube entered Titus's stomach, all of the gas and fluid collecting there would come rushing out. Stella did not want them rushing into her mouth.

The mark on the tube was eight inches from Titus's mouth, then six inches, then four. Stella shifted her attention to Titus's face.

Titus was following Stella's every movement with his piercing, sad brown eyes.

Stella knew she'd be in trouble if Titus resisted her. He was bigger than she was and much, much stronger. But Titus stood quietly and let Stella work. She had the idea that he knew she was trying to help him. Or perhaps he just didn't want to do anything to hurt her.

The mark on the tube was three inches from Titus's mouth. Stella couldn't push it in any farther. She blew a little harder. She twisted the tube to the left. She twisted it to the right. It wouldn't budge.

"What's the matter?" Papa Pete asked.

"It won't go in," Stella said, sitting back on her heels.

"Keep trying," Papa Pete said.

Stella set her shoulders and breathed in deeply. This time she blew harder than she had dared to before. She patiently turned the tube back and forth. She heard the minute hand on Anya's waiting room clock tick forward. The tube wasn't going in.

"I can't get it," Stella finally said.

"Don't be a quitter," Papa Pete said.

"I'm not quitting," Stella snapped. "It might not be possible to get the tube in. His stomach could be twisted."

"Maybe you're doing it wrong," Mr. Forester said.

"Do you want to try?" Stella demanded.

Mr. Forester held up his hands. "No, no! Sorry."

"I know how to do this," Stella told Papa Pete. "I did it dozens of times on Rufus."

Papa Pete nodded. "Now what? Titus looks worse."

He was right. The skin on Titus's stomach was drum tight. He seemed less alert, too. He looked tired standing there.

"I don't know," Stella admitted. "I only read half of the directions."

Papa Pete held the paper out to her.

Stella sat down on the floor and began to skim the pages. She looked up and eyed the needle sitting on the reception desk. What the paper suggested she do made sense, but she wasn't sure if she had the nerve. Just thinking about it made her hands clammy.

Titus's legs began to shake. He spread out his feet, and fought to stay standing.

"He's about to go down," Papa Pete said in a warning tone.

Stella jumped up. She had to do something *now*. "Mr. Forester, I want you to go into my aunt's office and wait for us there."

"Why?" Mr. Forester demanded, slowly standing. "What are you going to do?"

"You don't want to know," Stella told him firmly. "Now go!"

Mr. Forester looked mournfully at Titus. Then he scuttled off down the hall. Stella heard the door to Anya's office close. Boris barked once and then settled down.

Stella picked up the needle. She looked at Titus and licked her lips.

Don't worry about hurting the dog, the directions read. *He will already be in too much pain to notice what you are about to do.*

Somehow Stella doubted that.

"Do you think you can keep him on his feet?" she asked Papa Pete.

"Probably not," Papa Pete admitted.

Stella knew she had to work quickly. She got down on her knees in front of Titus's left side. His bulging stomach was only inches from her face.

Just do it, Stella told herself. She felt woozy but she pushed the feeling away. Titus's knees were buckling. She was out of time.

Stella ran her fingers lightly over Titus's side until she felt his last rib. Her hands shook as she took the cap off the needle and raised it above her shoulder.

"What are you doing?" Papa Pete demanded.

Stella brought her arm down swiftly and stabbed the needle into Titus's stomach just to the left of his last rib. It went in easily—like a pin into a blister.

Amazingly, Titus didn't react.

SWOOO . . .

Stella fell back as air rushed out of Titus's stomach.

"Oh, phew-wee!" Stella said. The air smelled bad—like someone had just burped right into her face.

Papa Pete didn't react to the smell. He was staring at the needle bug-eyed.

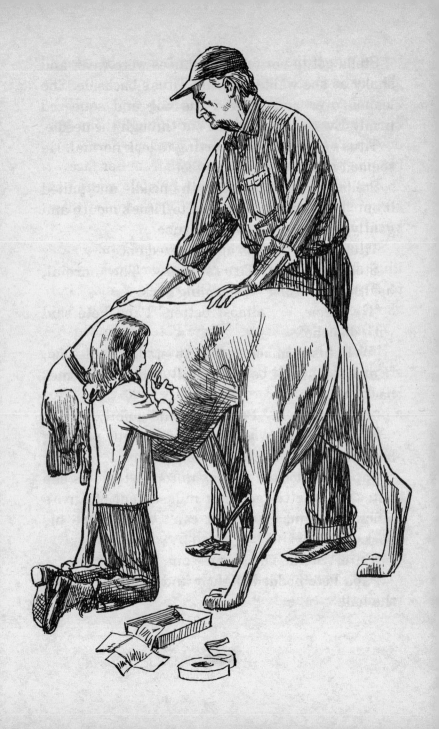

Stella got to her feet. Her knees were weak and shaky as she walked around Titus's backside. She leaned over and hugged the dog and squeezed firmly. Even more air came out through the needle.

Titus's stomach was starting to look normal. He seemed more stable on his feet.

Stella covered the end of the needle and pulled it out. Then she went around to Titus's mouth and gently removed the stomach tube.

Titus licked his lips and sneezed once.

Stella checked Titus's gums. The normal, healthy pink color was coming back.

"He seems . . . almost better," Papa Pete said with disbelief.

"Well, his stomach is still twisted," Stella said. "But I think he'll be okay until Aunt Anya comes back."

"Thanks to you," Papa Pete said quietly.

Stella blinked. Was Papa Pete actually praising her? She couldn't think of what to say.

Papa Pete looked just as uncomfortable as she felt. "You'd better get that milksop out of Anya's office," he said gruffly. "I can't wait to see his backside."

"Sure," Stella said. "And—um, thanks."

Papa Pete nodded slightly and Stella fled down the hall.

• 12 •

"Mr. Forester, you can come out now," Stella said, opening the door to Anya's office a crack.

Mr. Forester was sitting in Anya's swivel chair. He was leaning forward and clutching his stomach. "What happened?" he whispered, slowly lifting his eyes from the floor and searching Stella's face.

"Come see," Stella said gently. She took Mr. Forester's clammy hand and led him into the waiting room. Titus walked over and stood next to his owner. He even managed a halfhearted wag of his tail.

Mr. Forester dropped to his knees. He hugged

Titus around the chest. "Oh baby, I'm so happy you're okay!" he exclaimed in a shaky voice. He was smiling and tears were dripping on his chin.

Stella sent Mr. Forester home. She got Titus settled in the boarder room. She checked on the dachshund. He lifted his head and watched her curiously. He seemed fine. The next day, Anya could check with the sheriff's department and find out who owned the mobile home where Papa Pete had found him. His owners must be worried.

Merlin's cage was on the other side of the room. Stella crossed to him. Marisa's cat was stretched out on his side, sleeping soundly. He looked a bit too loose-limbed. Not neatly tucked together the way cats usually are.

Stella watched him breathe in and out. She felt uneasy, like she was keeping a secret from Marisa. True, the phones were out. But Stella still felt as if she were sneaking around. Marisa and Mrs. Capra had to be freaking out.

"I'll call as soon as Mom gets back," Stella promised herself. She turned out the light in the boarder room and went up the stairs.

Stella slid into Anya's bed and closed her eyes. It felt like hours later when she felt someone crawl into bed beside her.

"Aunt Anya?"

"No, it's me," Norma said.

"What time is it?"

"A little past two," Norma said. She put her head down on the pillow and let out a contented sigh.

"Did you get Anya?"

"Yeah," Norma said sleepily. "She was half frozen. She's sleeping down in the boarder room."

"Did she look at Merlin?" Stella asked anxiously.

"Yeah. Her expert opinion"—Norma interrupted herself for an enormous yawn—"is that he's going to be okay."

Stella sat up in bed, feeling wide awake. "Mom, can I use your cell phone?"

"*May* I," Norma corrected her.

"I want to call the Capras about Merlin," Stella said. "I know they won't mind."

"That's probably true," Norma said with a little laugh. She didn't say anything more for a long time.

"Does that mean it's okay?" Stella asked.

Norma didn't answer.

Stella studied her mother in the darkness. Her eyes were closed and her mouth was slightly open. She was breathing slowly and steadily. Stella crawled out of bed and found Norma's purse on the floor next to her shoes. She pulled out the cell phone, turned it on, and quickly dialed.

The phone rang once.

"Belle's Bed and Breakfast." Mrs. Capra sounded 101 percent alert.

"Mrs. Capra, it's Stella. Sorry to call so late. The phones at the clinic are down—"

"Tell me something I don't know!" Mrs. Capra exclaimed. "I've been calling every half hour all day. How's Merlin?"

Stella heard someone pick up another extension. "I'm here, too," Marisa said. She didn't sound as if she'd just crawled out of bed. "How's Merlin?"

"Mom and I had to operate on him," Stella blurted out. "Aunt Anya was stuck in Chico Hot Springs and the tinsel messed up his bowel. I—I'm sorry. It would have been better if Anya had operated when he first came in. Are you mad?" Stella braced herself for hysterics.

"Mad?" Mrs. Capra said faintly.

"All I care about is Merlin," Marisa said stoutly. "The important thing is that he's okay."

"Aunt Anya checked him over as soon as she got back," Stella said. "I think he's fine. I'm sure Aunt Anya will call you first thing in the morning."

"Thanks, Stella," Mrs. Capra said.

"Yeah," Marisa added. "I'm really glad you were there!"

Stella felt a bit faint as she said good night and turned off the phone. She'd never expected the Capras to thank her. She was glad Marisa wasn't mad at her.

For a moment, Stella sat staring at the door to Anya's closet. Then she made up her mind and dialed the phone again. She felt a rush of relief when the call went through, but her relief vanished when her father picked up and muttered a very sleepy hello.

"Daddy, it's Stella."

"Stella!" Jack said, suddenly sounding much less sleepy. "Is everything okay?"

"Yes! Fine. Mom is here. She's asleep. I just need to talk to Cora."

"She's in bed. Why aren't *you* in bed?"

"I'll go to sleep in one second," Stella promised. "But could you wake Cora up? I promise it's really important."

"It better be," Jack growled. But he put down the phone and a few minutes later Cora picked up.

The next morning, Stella slipped out of bed just as the sun was coming up. Norma was curled up in the covers with a slight smile on her face.

Stella pulled on her clothes as quietly as possible. She picked up her boots and walked into the living room in her socks.

Papa Pete was snoring on the couch.

Stella left a note on Anya's kitchen table. She went quietly down the steps. She sat on the bottom step long enough to lace up her boots, and then eased out the front door.

The snow had finally stopped. Main Street was plowed, but the town seemed quieter than usual.

Cora was waiting for Stella in The Wooden Spoon parking lot. She was riding Cinnamon, her favorite horse from Jake's Stables. She was also leading Bay, the mare Stella had ridden a few days earlier.

"You ready?" Cora asked.

"Definitely," Stella said as she swung up onto Bay's back.

Cora turned Cinnamon and nudged him with her heels. They rode much faster than they had the other day. Stella had to pay attention to her posture and grip on the reins.

The girls took the familiar route to Jake's Stables. Then they followed their path from two days earlier. Stella kept her eyes open for a ranch house or the corral Norma had described.

In the snow it was impossible to tell where the

ranch ended and the park started. The only clue was a tumbled down fence that could have marked the rancher's land.

The girls rode for half an hour before Cora spotted a chimney in the distance. They headed toward it, moving slightly uphill. Stella had to urge Bay through the deep snow. Ten minutes later, they rode over a slight knoll and the ranch house came into view.

"There are the buffalo." Stella pointed to a shiny metal corral directly behind the ranch house.

"Great," Cora said. "We're going to get caught for sure." Her tone was slightly amused. Obviously, she didn't really care.

The girls were quiet as they surveyed the situation.

"I'll get the gate," Stella said after a moment.

"Open it and then get out of the way," Cora said. "Mom will be mad if you get hurt."

"You, too," Stella said.

"Hi-YA!" Cora yelled. Cinnamon galloped down the snowy ridge.

Bay hesitated and then followed. Stella loosened the reins and let Bay choose her own pace. The horse surged forward, straining to keep up with Cinnamon. Stella felt as if she were flying. Her heart was in her mouth—partly from the

speed and partly from fear of what she was about to do.

Stella was breathless by the time she pulled up even with the corral. She leaned sideways in her saddle, unlatched the gate, and swung it open.

The buffalo—there were six of them, or maybe seven, it was hard to count them when they were all bunched together—watched curiously.

Cora rode past Stella and got behind the buffalo. "Haay-ya!" she yelled. She stood up in her saddle and waved her arms over her head.

The buffalo reacted quickly. They rose to their feet and moved toward the gate together. Bay shifted nervously under Stella as the massive buffalo thundered past in a blur of brown.

Cora rode up behind Stella. She was panting and she'd lost her hat, but she was grinning like mad. "That was fun!"

"I think we should follow them," Stella said. "Make sure they head into the park and don't double back."

"Think again." Cora's smile faded as she pointed toward the house.

An old woman had come out the back door. She was wearing a purple chenille bathrobe and cowboy boots. Stella cringed as the woman plunged into the snow and hobbled toward them, waving a golf club in the air and shouting.

"You kids stop right there!" she yelled. "Stop!" she repeated even though Stella and Cora weren't moving. "What are you doing on my land?"

Cora sat up straighter in her saddle. "We let the buffalo free!" she yelled back.

"You're trespassing!" the woman yelled. "I'm calling the sheriff's department. Get off those horses and tell me your names. I'm going to call your parents."

Stella and Cora slipped out of their saddles. They led the horses toward the red-faced woman.

"You're in big trouble now!" the woman yelled.

Stella knew she was right. But as she looked out over the pasture and spotted the buffalo plowing their way through the snow, she didn't care.

Some things are worth a little trouble.

THE AMAZING STORY OF
LLLUCKY BOO

Lllucky Boo (yes—that really is how you spell his name) may be one of the luckiest dogs in the world. His family includes two dog-loving kids, a veterinarian "dad," and a "mom" nice enough to carry him in a snuggly when he's tired. Lllucky lives on a ranch in Idaho with plenty of space to run and lots of dogs, cats, and horses to play with. Nobody seems to mind that Lllucky has just three legs, a crooked tail, and a few missing teeth.

Ten-year-old Lex Becker told us his dog's story. "Lllucky was playing in a train yard and his front right leg got run over by a train." Lllucky probably tried to get back home, but the train was still racing by and it blocked his way. Eventually, Lllucky wandered into a nearby Canadian border station. His leg was such a mess that the people at the station couldn't decide what to do. Some wanted to shoot the dog. Others wanted to help him.

"They finally agreed to call his owner," Lex told us. "She said to put him out of his misery, but they decided not to. One woman lifted him into the back of her truck. She was taking him to the veterinarian in town. But Lllucky jumped out of her pickup!"

The pickup was going 65 miles an hour. Lllucky hit the road hard and landed in dense bushes and trees. The people trying to rescue him couldn't find him. "They thought the coyotes would get him," Lex said.

The rescuers weren't ready to let Lllucky be eaten by wild animals. One of them let his own dog loose. The dog led the rescuers to where Lllucky was trying to get a drink out of a creek. The rescuers got Lllucky back to the truck and managed to transport him safely to the veterinarian. The vet amputated Lllucky's leg and took the dog to a nearby animal shelter where he waited for someone to adopt him.

Lex's parents, Marty and Teresa Becker, read about Lllucky in the local papers. The dog was living with a temporary foster family. The family's three-year-old daughter named him "Lucky Boo" because he had so many boo-boos.

Lllucky's story touched the Beckers, so they were surprised when six weeks went by and nobody offered the resilient dog a permanent home. They decided to go meet him.

"He came bounding up to us," Marty remembered. "He tried to put his imaginary paw up on Teresa's leg. He laid his head on her lap." After that greeting, the Beckers couldn't resist taking Lllucky home.

So what's it like having a three-legged dog? Lex pondered that question for a while. "Lllucky can't walk up our barn stairs," he finally offered, "because our barn stairs are really steep. But that's about the only thing he can't do."

Marty explained the final mystery. "We changed the spelling of his name so that it had three Ls," he said. "They stand for *lost* his leg, *leaped* from a truck, and got *lost* in the woods."

Lllucky is a fortunate dog because he survived all of his injuries and because he found a loving home. According to **Petopia.com**, shelters put to sleep—or euthanize—about five million *healthy* animals (mostly dogs and cats) each year. Animals that are old, sick, or disabled have a very small chance of finding a home.

How you can help

Here are some things you can do to make sure the stories of more homeless dogs and cats have happy endings:

- Support the Million Pet Mission sponsored by the authors of *Chicken Soup for the Pet Lover's Soul* (including Lllucky's owner, Marty Becker), Petopia, and the ASPCA by welcoming a homeless pet into your home. Start the search for the pet of your dreams by visiting **Petfinder.com**. This website allows you to search shelters near your home by type of animal, breed, age, and size.
- Have your veterinarian fix your dogs and cats so that they can't have puppies or kittens. This will help reduce the number of unwanted animals in shelters.
- Behavior problems are a top reason people abandon pets. Make sure you have well-behaved pets by training them. Don't give up on an old dog or cat! Even older animals can learn new tricks. Ask your veterinarian for help with stubborn behavior problems.
- Consider taking in a pet other people may reject because it is a mixed breed, has a disability, or is old. You can read more about the

benefits of adopting an old dog at **www.sr dogs.com**.

- Take any stray animals you find to a shelter committed to finding homes for all of the animals they receive.
- Show people that you're proud of your mixed-breed dog. Participate in events sponsored by May Day for Mutts, a nationwide organization.

Emily Costello, the author of the *Animal Emergency* series, would like to hear about your pet and what makes it special. Send her an e-mail at **emily@enarch-ma.com** or write to her care of HarperCollins Children's Books.